MAGNUS *at the* FIRE

by JENNIFER ARMSTRONG   *illustrated by* OWEN SMITH

SIMON & SCHUSTER BOOKS FOR YOUNG READERS
New York London Toronto Sydney

Magnus had been a fire horse at the Broadway Firehouse in Hope Springs for ten good years. For ten years he had plenty of oats, clean straw, and good water, and the firemen always had a kind word or an apple for him. Beside him in their own stalls were his partners, Billy and Sparks. They were three big grays, strong as oxen and fast as the wind.

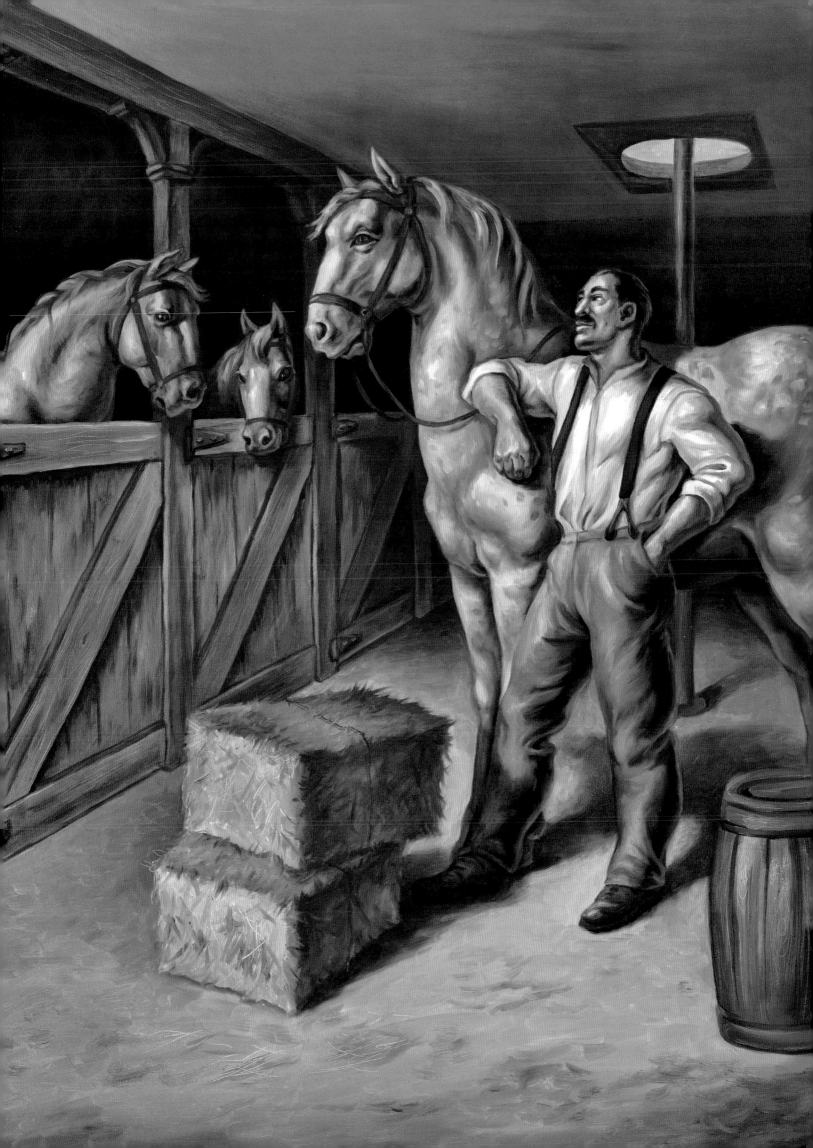

Whenever the bell set out clanging from the top of the firehouse, Magnus, Billy, and Sparks sprang into action. An automatic switch opened the gate in front of their stalls and dropped their harnesses onto their backs. As soon as each horse felt it thump into place, he stepped forward into his yoke and one of the firemen buckled it up.

In thirty seconds Magnus and his partners were ready to roll, and together they raced with the heavy steam pumper to the fire. Everyone stood back in awe as the three mighty fire horses galloped along.

"Pegasus himself couldn't beat those grays!" folks always said. "Look at 'em fly!"

No matter how hot and wild the fire was, or how many people were yelling and screaming, or how many dogs were barking, Magnus was never afraid. Being a fire horse was his whole life. He had even gone to the horse college outside of Germanville, so he knew how to handle himself around calamity and chaos. He stood rock steady while the firemen put out the fire. Then he pulled the pumper back to the Broadway Firehouse and had a rubdown and an extra measure of oats. Being a fire horse was a hard job, but it had its rewards. Little children wandered into the firehouse every day just to give Magnus sugar lumps, and dug their elbows into each other's sides as they said, "That's a mighty swell fire horse. He's a real live hero."

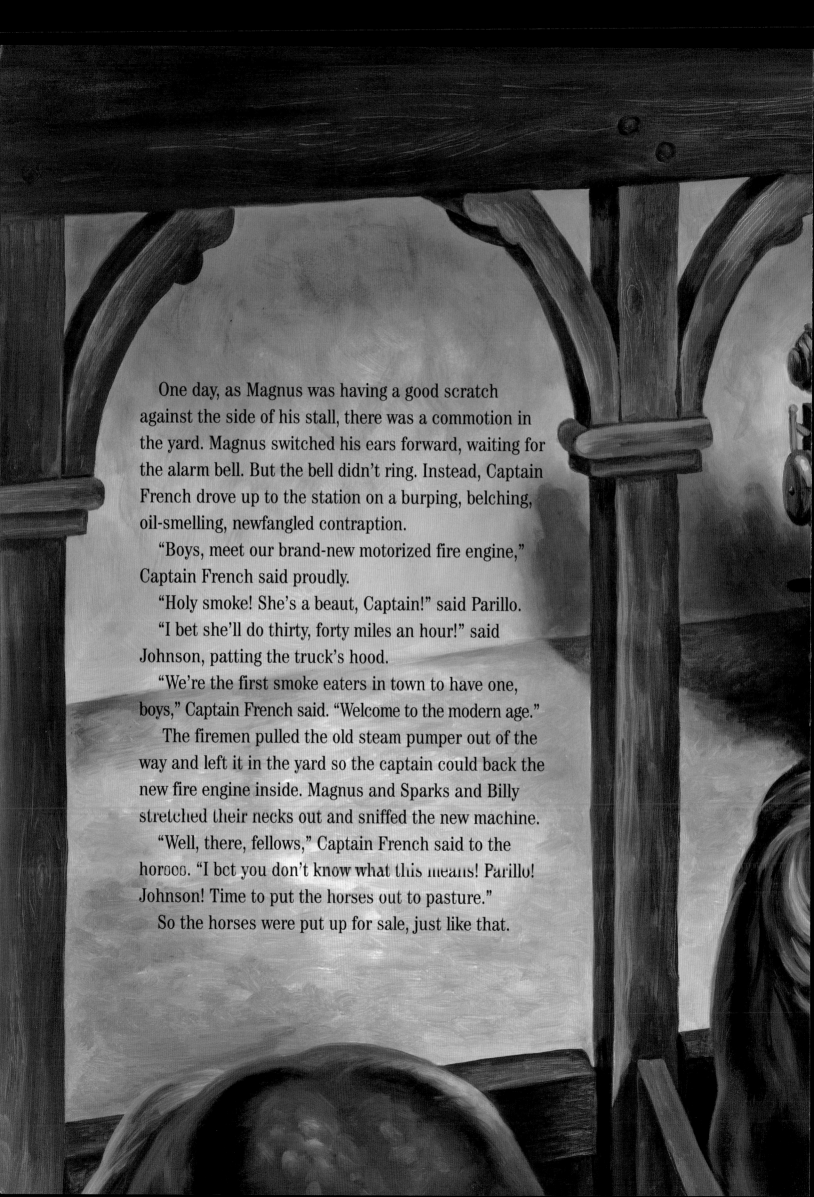

One day, as Magnus was having a good scratch against the side of his stall, there was a commotion in the yard. Magnus switched his ears forward, waiting for the alarm bell. But the bell didn't ring. Instead, Captain French drove up to the station on a burping, belching, oil-smelling, newfangled contraption.

"Boys, meet our brand-new motorized fire engine," Captain French said proudly.

"Holy smoke! She's a beaut, Captain!" said Parillo.

"I bet she'll do thirty, forty miles an hour!" said Johnson, patting the truck's hood.

"We're the first smoke eaters in town to have one, boys," Captain French said. "Welcome to the modern age."

The firemen pulled the old steam pumper out of the way and left it in the yard so the captain could back the new fire engine inside. Magnus and Sparks and Billy stretched their necks out and sniffed the new machine.

"Well, there, fellows," Captain French said to the horses. "I bet you don't know what this means! Parillo! Johnson! Time to put the horses out to pasture."

So the horses were put up for sale, just like that.

The next day, Billy left to work at the dairy delivering milk and butter. For a week, Magnus and Sparks took a great deal of pleasure and enjoyment from the little bit of pasture behind the firehouse, where he and Sparks could roll in the grass to scratch their backs any old time they wanted, and they could bask in the sun with their eyes shut, whisking flies with their tails.

But the next time the bell began to peal from the firehouse roof, Magnus dashed to the gate, waiting for the drop of the automatic harness onto his back. He sniffed the air for smoke and trembled with anticipation.

While Magnus stood by the gate, the new fire truck rumbled out of the firehouse with its bell banging away, and the firemen drove off without him. Magnus waited and waited to go to the fire and do his job, just the way he'd done it for ten years.

Later, when the truck came rumbling back, Magnus smelled the smoke on the firemen's clothes. They had been to a fire without him. He stayed there for a while longer, smelling the smoke, and then finally, wandered back into the pasture.

The next time the fire bell began clanging from the roof, Magnus didn't wait to be left behind, no sir. The big old horse backed up for a running start, and then sprang clear over the fence. He followed the smell of smoke, galloping down Long Alley and over another two fences, his mane and tail flaring out behind him like flames until he reached the fire at the oyster house on Congress Street. He was standing there, breathing hard, when the fire truck arrived.

"What in blazes is Magnus doing here?" Captain French demanded.

Of course, Magnus couldn't help getting in the way, and he didn't quite know what to do without the pumper to pull. Once the fire was dead, Parillo led Magnus back to the firehouse and put him in the pasture with Sparks.

The next day, a carpenter came to make the pasture fence higher. Magnus and the firemen were watching him when Zeke Fancher, the old captain, came by the firehouse for a visit. He lived on his son's apple farm now, but he missed the excitement and romance of being a smoke eater.

"Guess what old Magnus did yesterday," Parillo said. "Jumped the fence and beat us to the fire. Crazy horse."

"You don't say?" asked Fancher. He patted Magnus's neck and gave him an apple. "I know how you feel, old-timer," he whispered in the big horse's ear.

It wasn't too many days later that Magnus answered the call again. Of course, he had to bust down part of the new fence to do it, but when the fire truck arrived at the fire, sure enough, Magnus was already there.

"You darned stubborn horse!" Captain French hollered. "We don't need you anymore! Somebody get Magnus out of the way! We're trying to fight a fire here!"

Magnus and the firemen hadn't been back at the Broadway Firehouse more than five hours when there was another alarm. The bell clanged, Parillo gunned the truck, and the firemen tore out of the firehouse, horns blasting.

Even as they barreled down the street, they saw Magnus sail over the fence and come charging behind them.

"We've got to do something about that horse!" French shouted. "He's getting to be a real troublemaker! Why won't he just stay retired and keep out of the way?"

Thick smoke was pouring out of the windows of the United States Hotel. The firemen could see it as the truck barreled down Broadway, but just as they passed Gilbert's Barbershop, there was a sound like a cannon shot. The truck skidded and swerved to a stop and black smoke belched out from under the hood.

Captain French threw his helmet on the ground. "Blew the motor! Darned machine!"

"We're not close enough!" Parillo warned. "We have to get closer!"

The firemen poured out of the truck and tried to push it up the street. But the new motorized engine was so heavy that they couldn't budge it more than an inch. Men from the barbershop and nearby hotels dashed out to help push, but there wasn't enough room for everyone to get a handhold. They just couldn't do it. The fire was growing wilder every second. Smoke and sparks swirled up in the hot air, and folks were stumbling out of the hotel, coughing and choking and wailing for help.

"It's no use!" Captain French bellowed. "Go get Magnus!"

Johnson ran up the street to the burning hotel and, sure enough, there was Magnus watching the fire.

"Come on, fella, step lively." Johnson grabbed the big horse's halter and ran him back down Broadway to the busted fire truck.

Parillo and Stevens rigged up a harness for Magnus with a hose.

"Go, Magnus!" Parillo said with a smack to the horse's rump.

Magnus felt the tug of the weight behind him when he lunged forward. The truck was pretty heavy, and he didn't have Sparks and Billy to help him pull. But he dug in with his big hooves, fighting for a foothold.

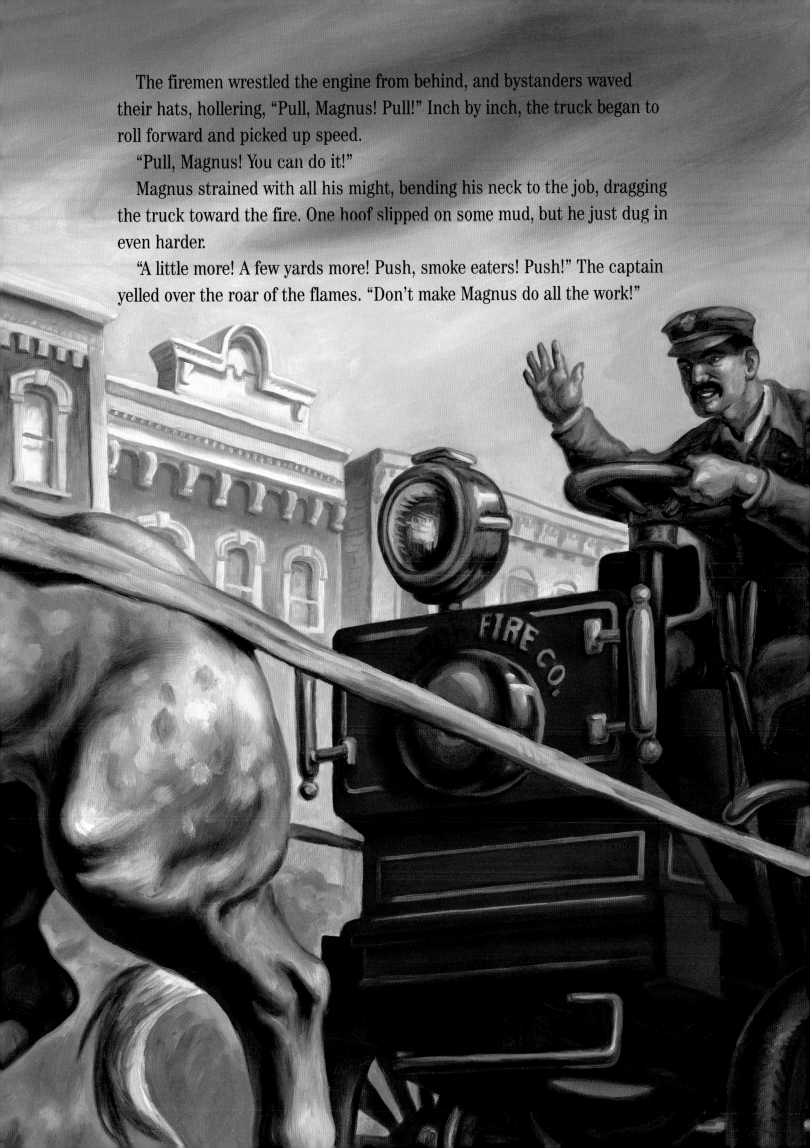

The firemen wrestled the engine from behind, and bystanders waved their hats, hollering, "Pull, Magnus! Pull!" Inch by inch, the truck began to roll forward and picked up speed.

"Pull, Magnus! You can do it!"

Magnus strained with all his might, bending his neck to the job, dragging the truck toward the fire. One hoof slipped on some mud, but he just dug in even harder.

"A little more! A few yards more! Push, smoke eaters! Push!" The captain yelled over the roar of the flames. "Don't make Magnus do all the work!"

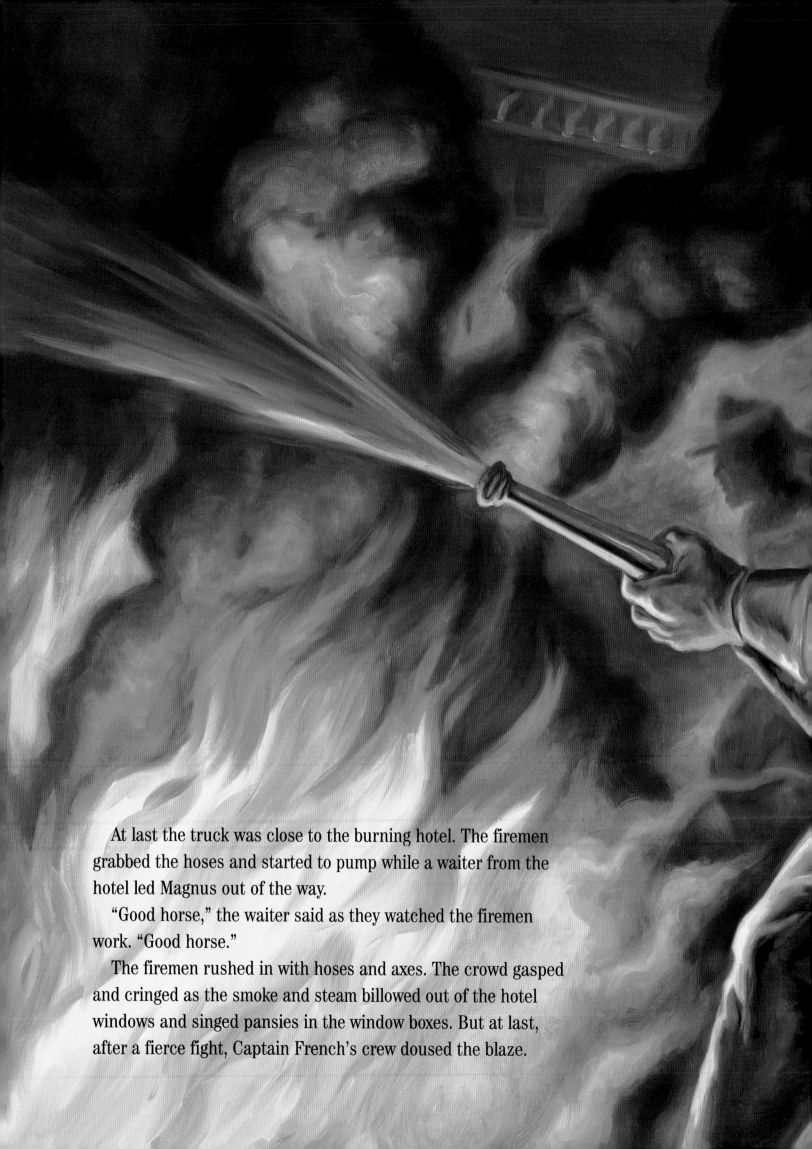

At last the truck was close to the burning hotel. The firemen grabbed the hoses and started to pump while a waiter from the hotel led Magnus out of the way.

"Good horse," the waiter said as they watched the firemen work. "Good horse."

The firemen rushed in with hoses and axes. The crowd gasped and cringed as the smoke and steam billowed out of the hotel windows and singed pansies in the window boxes. But at last, after a fierce fight, Captain French's crew doused the blaze.

Exhausted and covered with soot, the firemen and Magnus walked back to the firehouse. "Good horse," Johnson said as he rubbed Magnus down. "Brave horse."

The next day, old Captain Fancher came to the Broadway Firehouse and led Magnus back home with him. "We're going somewhere you won't hear the bell, old smoke eater. You don't have to answer it anymore. You've earned your rest."

So from then on Magnus spent his days eating apples and pulling Fancher's grandkids around the orchard in a wagon, and they had grand times when they held autumn bonfires behind the barn. Sometimes the old captain's daughter-in-law rang a bell to call the children in to supper. And pretty soon Magnus learned that the sound of the bell meant one last hug from all the kids before they ran inside, where the fire in the stove was nice and warm.

For fine, fine horses everywhere—J. A.

To August, Walden, and Liz—O. S.

✦ A Note to the Reader ✦

The use of horses in firefighting became widespread during the 1800s after advancements in steam power led to the invention of the steam-powered fire engine. Before that time, fires were fought by volunteers who passed buckets of water or used small hand-powered pumpers that they had pulled to the site. When the much larger steam pumpers began to be used, firefighters quickly realized that these gigantic "engines" were much too heavy to be pulled by hand. (Some weighed as much as sixteen thousand pounds!) So they began to use horses. This worked great! And for decades—until around 1900—horses were sent to special schools and trained to respond to fires in much the same way as Magnus does in this story. These horses were seen as heroes in their communities. They were cheered and adored. They were visited and pampered.

Then shortly after 1900 all of that changed. A less expensive alternative to horse-drawn engines arrived on the scene in the form of self-propelled fire engines. The monstrous vehicle used in this book, built by the Waterous Engine Works in 1906, is generally believed to be one of the first. And while these new engines didn't start out being as dependable as the horse teams they replaced, the cost benefit quickly became very apparent. By 1910 the Fire Department of New York noted that a team of horses cost six hundred and sixty dollars a year to maintain, but a comparable new automotive engine cost only eighty-five dollars. By the end of the 1920s horse-drawn fire engines were a thing of the past.

Happily, these heroic horses almost always found wonderful new homes and jobs. And history is littered with accounts of these fine, stalwart horses whisking their new, often unsuspecting, owners to fires whenever they heard the clanging from the top of the firehouse calling them to duty.

SIMON & SCHUSTER BOOKS FOR YOUNG READERS

An imprint of Simon & Schuster Children's Publishing Division

1230 Avenue of the Americas, New York, New York 10020

Text copyright © 2005 by Jennifer Armstrong

Illustrations copyright © 2005 by Owen Smith

All rights reserved, including the right of reproduction in whole or in part in any form.

SIMON & SCHUSTER BOOKS FOR YOUNG READERS is a trademark of Simon & Schuster, Inc.

Book design by Greg Stadnyk

The text for this book is set in Century

The illustrations for this book are rendered in oil paint.

Manufactured in China

2 4 6 8 10 9 7 5 3 1

Library of Congress Cataloging-in-Publication Data

Armstrong, Jennifer, 1961–

Magnus at the fire / Jennifer Armstrong ; illustrated by Owen Smith.

p. cm.

Summary: When the Broadway Firehouse acquires a motorized fire engine, Magnus the fire horse is not ready to retire.

ISBN 0-689-83922-7

[1. Horses—Fiction. 2. Fire extinction—Fiction. 3. Fire engines—Fiction.] I. Smith, Owen, 1964– ill. II. Title.

PZ7.A73367Mag 2005

[E]—dc22   2004011487

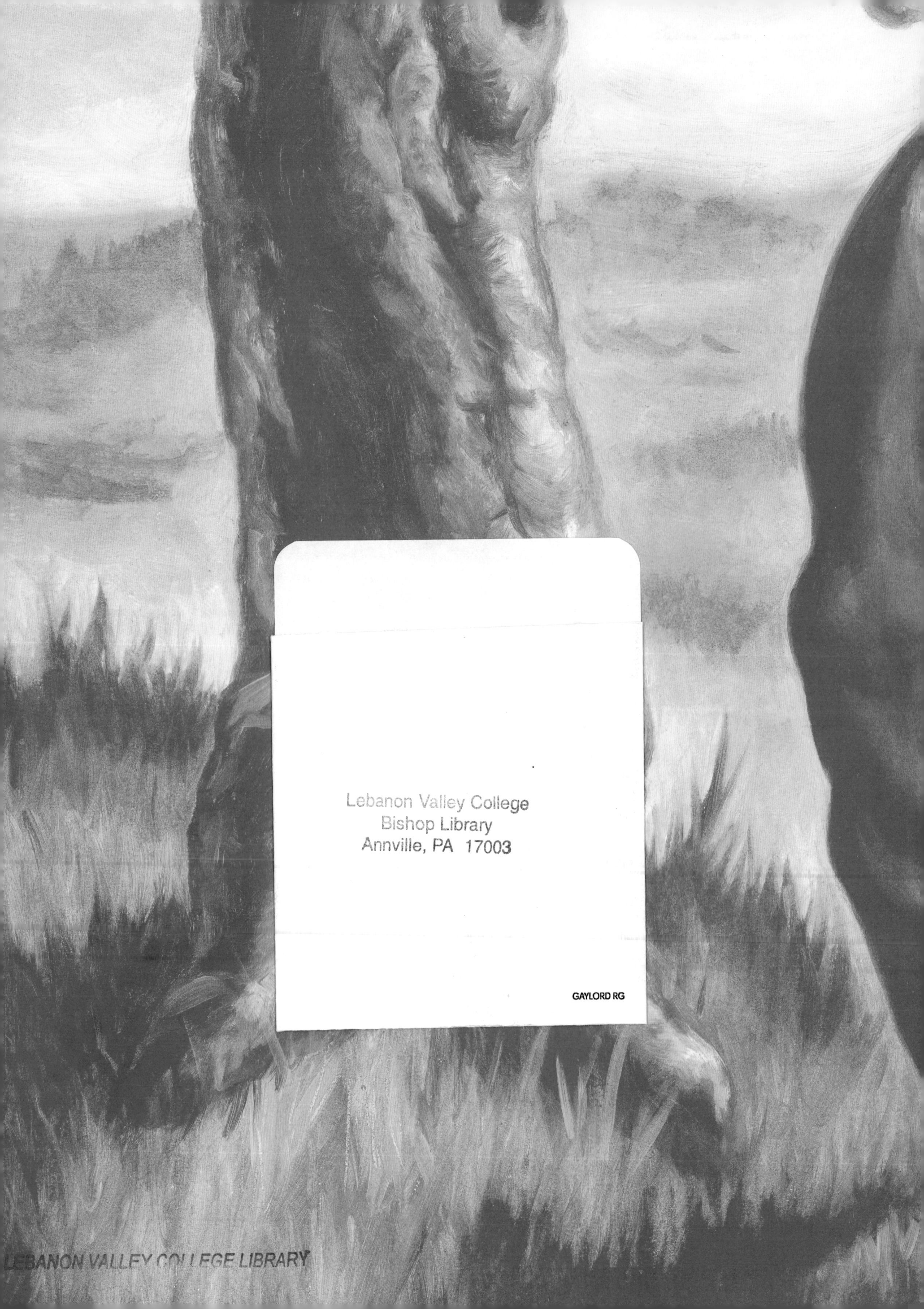